DALMATIANS

Escape from
De Vil Mansion

Adapted from the live-action film by

Gabrielle Charbonnet

DISNEP
PRESS

New York

Printed in the United States of America.

First Edition

1 3 5 7 9 10 8 6 4 2

This book is set in 16-point. Berkeley Book

Library of Congress Catalog Card Number: 96-84826

ISBN: 0-7868-4109-5

Contents

1

A Scream in the Night

"They're here! I've got them!"
When Wizzer heard Nanny's voice,
he raced to the front door. Nanny
was one of his favorite humans.
Fourteen other Dalmatian puppies, Wizzer's brothers and sisters,
shot past him. Wizzer jumped up on
Nanny's ankles and yipped. She smiled at him.
"To the kitchen!" she said. "Everyone!"
Wizzer's mother, Perdy, trotted downstairs
and followed the puppies and Nanny into the

kitchen. Pongo, Wizzer's father, joined them. Roger and Anita, the household humans, pushed through the door.

Nanny placed a large package on the table, and Anita opened it. She took out a red leather dog collar. "Jewel?" Jewel was one of Wizzer's sisters. She stepped forward, and Anita carefully buckled the pretty collar around her neck.

"Dipstick?" said Roger. Dipstick got a collar, too.

One by one, all the puppies got their collars. Wizzer waited for his turn. It was taking forever. He needed to go outside, but there was no way he could leave the fun.

Finally, even though he *knew* he wasn't supposed to, he piddled under the table. What a relief. But only babies piddled inside. Mom and Dad kept telling him that.

"Wizzer?" said Roger.

Feeling very embarrassed, Wizzer crept forward and got his handsome new collar with his name on it.

"I'll get the mop," Nanny said.

That night, Wizzer curled up with his brothers and sisters in their big bed under the kitchen sink. He yawned and scratched behind his ear. His foot hit his new collar. It would take him a while to get used to it. But he was very proud of it. It made him look so grown-up, just like his dad.

Wizzer was almost asleep when Pongo and Perdy came to tuck the puppies in. He felt his mom's cool nose nudging him. He wiggled happily. Mom and Dad were about to go for their late-night walk with their humans. Wizzer snuggled up to Two-Tone as he heard his parents leave.

"Somebody didn't finish their supper," Nanny said. "We can't waste food."

Through a crack in the curtain, Wizzer saw Nanny scrape some leftover dog food into a container. Then the doorbell rang. Wizzer yawned again. Maybe the humans had forgotten their keys.

Nanny's quick steps headed toward the door. Wizzer buried his nose under one paw.

Crash! The sound of breaking wood jolted Wizzer awake. Nanny screamed— once, twice, three times!

Wizzer leaped up and poked his nose out of the sink curtain. He barked as loud as he could. Whatever the trouble was, he was going to meet it head-on!

2

Kidnapped!

Wizzer's brothers and sisters tumbled out of their warm bed and hid in fear behind him. Wizzer wasn't afraid. He barked again, warning the strangers that they would have to deal with him first, before they got to his brothers and sisters.

The sink curtains were jerked aside. A bony hand reached through. Wizzer sank his little teeth into it, as hard as he could.

The hand pulled him for-ward, and Wizzer saw that he was biting a tall, thin man with a beard and mustache. The man easily shook 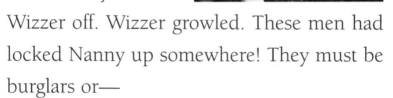 Wizzer off. Wizzer growled. These men had locked Nanny up somewhere! They must be burglars or—

"The bag, Horace!" the man said.

A short, fat man, dressed in shabby clothes, held open a large sack.

The tall man reached under the sink and grabbed Lucky. As Wizzer watched in horror, the man threw Lucky into the sack. After Lucky went the other puppies, one by one.

Wizzer was the last, and even though he fought bravely, the man chucked him into the bag with the rest.

"That's the lot," the man said. "Let's get out of here."

Inside the sack it was dark and crowded. Wizzer could tell his brothers and sisters were scared. Several of them were whimpering. The man lifted the sack high and they all tumbled over one another.

The two men were talking, but Wizzer couldn't make out what they were saying. He could hear Nanny screaming and pounding against a door.

What was happening? Who were these two bad men? Wizzer's parents were going to be *soooo* mad when they got home with their humans and found their puppies missing.

Mom and Dad were very strict about the puppies' not going off on their own. They always said you never knew what could happen. There were bad people out there, people like Cruella De Vil.

Wizzer didn't know if Cruella De Vil had anything to do with the puppies' kidnapping. But he did know that the men had opened the door and taken them outside. Cold air blew through the thin cloth bag. Jewel was crying loudly as the bag bounced along. Most of the other puppies were crying, too. Wizzer tried to bite his way out of the sack. But he could hardly move.

"Woof!" A loud bark sounded very close.

Wizzer had heard that bark before. It was the bulldog who lived on the other side of the park. He had asked what was going on. Why were the puppies crying? Where were Pongo and Perdy?

Before Wizzer could answer, a voice told the dog, "Montgomery! Heel, boy!"

Then the sack went flying through the

10

air, and the puppies landed on a cold metal surface.

Large doors clanged shut. There was only blackness and coldness.

Wizzer could still hear the bulldog's barking. It sounded like he was going to try to get a message to Wizzer's mom and dad. But the rest of what he was saying was lost as a large motor started.

Wizzer opened his eyes wide. They were inside a truck! But where were they going?

3

Kipper to the Rescue

For what seemed like hours, the truck bumped and rattled over winding roads. Wizzer told the other puppies not to worry. Their parents would come after them, or they would escape somehow. But, inside, he wasn't so sure.

Suddenly the truck stopped and Wizzer felt a gust of cold air. The puppies tumbled over one another as one of the bad men flung the sack over his shoulder. Wizzer heard a wooden door creak, and then—*oof!* The puppies were tossed to the floor.

Wizzer bravely stepped out of the sack. He looked around at the strange place he, his brothers, and his sisters were in. It was the

very large library of a run-down old mansion. The room was crowded with broken and dusty furniture. Tall bookcases lined the walls, moldy books filling their shelves.

Wizzer had never seen anything like it.

But the most amazing thing was . . . the other puppies. As Wizzer's brothers and sisters crept from the bag, puppies poked their noses out from behind furniture and from under old newspapers and magazines.

There were more puppies than Wizzer could even begin to count. Puppies sat on couches and chairs; puppies slept on carpets; puppies chewed on books. Everywhere

Wizzer looked, it was puppies, puppies, puppies. *And they were all Dalmatians.*

The other puppies had no idea why they had been brought here or what was going to happen. Wizzer and his brothers and sisters were the only ones wearing collars.

After meeting most of the others, Wizzer and his family curled up together on an old sofa, worried, tired, and scared.

Wizzer put his head down on his paws. Then he heard a scratching sound, followed by a small creak and a *thunk*!

Wizzer slowly stood up, peeking over the arm of the sofa. Across the room, an old grate had come off the wall and fallen to the floor. As Wizzer watched, one paw, and then another, poked through the opening.

The paws belonged to a small brown dog.

Wizzer had never seen him before.

The strange dog, whose name was Kipper, moved through the crowd of puppies. He quietly explained that he was part of a rescue team. The puppies had to come with him quickly, before the two bad guys came back.

Rescued! Wizzer thought happily. What an adventure!

Kipper led the puppies out through the hole one by one. The grate hole led to the parlor. After the parlor, Kipper explained, they would have to go up a long staircase.

Finally the last puppy squeezed through

the hole. Wizzer huddled with the others in the shadows along the walls. Kipper led the puppies through the parlor. Suddenly he froze.

Wizzer heard heavy footsteps coming toward them. He sank farther into the shadows. Horace—the short, fat man—appeared in the doorway. The puppies held their breath. If he found them now, it was all over.

Horace looked around the room suspiciously. He glanced across at the closed library doors. Looking puzzled, he left the parlor and went down the hall.

Whew. That had been close. Kipper led the puppies toward the parlor door again.

It wouldn't be long now, Wizzer thought. They just had to stick to the plan.

Bump! Behind Wizzer, a puppy slipped and slid into a small table. The puppy looked up in fear. An old, dust-covered lamp teetered on the table edge. The lamp rocked back and forth. Then it tumbled to the ground, breaking with a loud *crash!*

4

Another Escape Attempt

Like a school of furry, spotted fish, the puppies turned and raced back to the grate opening. They poured through the hole back into the library as fast as they could, with Kipper hurrying them on.

Outside the parlor, Wizzer heard the ripping sound of wood being torn apart. He heard a man say, "Horace?"

Footsteps came into the parlor. Wizzer

leaped through the grate, followed by the last three puppies and then Kipper. The puppies hid Kipper just one second before the tall library doors burst open. The man with the beard—whose name was Jasper—stood there, holding a wooden stair railing. He stared at the puppies with mean eyes.

Wizzer tried to act as if nothing had happened, though his heart was beating like a drum. He yawned. He licked a paw. He scratched behind his ear.

After another mean look, Jasper left the library, locking the doors behind him.

Kipper rose up from where he had been

hiding—under a tangled pile of puppies. Jewel was sitting on his head.

Kipper and the puppies waited for the right moment to try another escape. They heard Horace and Jasper stomping around in the entry, and once they heard the two men yell. Several loud thumps and bumps followed the yell, and then all was quiet.

It was some time later when the library doors opened. Horace came into the room. The puppies cowered—Wizzer remembered how Horace and Jasper had thrown them into the truck.

Horace grinned down at them. Wizzer wanted to bite him on the ankles. A puppy—Wizzer didn't know his name—was sitting on the floor in front of Horace.

"Hungry?" Horace asked.

The puppy looked at him sadly. They were all hungry. The men hadn't fed them.

"I brung ya something to eat," said Horace. Horace brought out a wire mousetrap, baited with cheese. He set it on the floor in front of the puppy and laughed.

It took all of Wizzer's self-control not to go over and chomp down on Horace's hand as hard as he could. Of course the puppy couldn't eat the cheese—not without getting his nose snapped by the strong wire trap.

Jasper came into the library. "What're you doing?" he asked Horace. "I asked you to check on the mutts. Not keep 'em company."

Horace pointed to the mousetrap. "Look."

Jasper grabbed Horace's arm, yanking him out of the library. The doors slammed shut behind them. Several puppies gathered around the cheese, licking their chops. Wizzer growled angrily.

In no time, Kipper had organized the puppies again. As they did before, they started hopping through the hole into the parlor, one by one. They moved quickly and quietly and hid in the shadows along the walls.

Kipper led the way to the entry hall. As Wizzer got closer to the doorway, he could hear Jasper calling, "Hello? Anybody there?"

Right outside the parlor door was a huge staircase, covered with a rotting carpet. Cobwebs coated the crooked banisters. Kipper started up the stairs, the line of puppies following him. The stairs were tall, and the puppies short, so they had to hop from step to step. Peeking around the parlor door, where he waited with the others, Wizzer could see the carpet sagging under the weight of the puppies. Some of the steps must be broken, he figured.

Kipper waited on the landing, pressing puppies onward and upward. Wizzer heard the mansion's front door shut.

"Maybe we was hearing things," Horace said.

Wizzer swallowed hard. Jasper and

Horace were coming down the hall! In another few steps, they would spot the puppies! Then a loud horn honked outside. The footsteps turned and headed back to the front door. Wizzer sighed with relief.

Soon the last of the puppies was hopping up the stairs. As Wizzer trotted across the entryway, he spotted a magazine lying on the floor. There was a picture of a woman

wearing a fur coat and holding a cigarette lighter. It had been hours since Wizzer had been outside. He just couldn't help himself. Hadn't Dad taught them to use paper when they had to "go" inside? Well, here was paper. Wizzer quickly piddled on the magazine.

The front door slammed shut again. The bad men were coming! Wizzer ran to the stairs and started climbing them as fast as he could.

5

Outwitting the Nitwits

Heavy boots pounded into the doorway. Two sharp white flashlight beams danced across the walls and came to rest on the stairs. They shined on Wizzer!

Gulping, Wizzer kept jumping up the steps. The flashlight beams then moved to shine on the group of puppies waiting on the landing. Other puppies climbed the rest of the stairs. Wizzer was the very last one.

"I don't believe me eyes," said Jasper.

Kipper ran downstairs, grabbed Wizzer by the scruff of the neck, and lifted him into the air. Although he was not much bigger than the puppy, he was very strong. Kipper bounded up the stairs with him.

"Drop that puppy!" Jasper yelled. "You lousy—" The two men charged for the stairs but suddenly cried out in surprise. When Wizzer looked down, he saw Jasper and Horace flying through the air. They landed on their backs, followed by pages of damp magazine and their flashlights.

The puppies scrambled up the rest of the stairs as fast as their little legs could go.

"Ruff! Ruff!" Kipper barked, urging them forward.

Downstairs, Horace and Jasper picked themselves up and headed toward the steps.

"I don't care what you say," Horace said. "I think we better be careful."

"You're afraid of puppies, now, Horace?" Jasper teased.

"It ain't about being afraid. It's about being careful."

"Careful of what?" Jasper asked.

Wizzer looked over his shoulder as he hopped up the stairs. The two bad men were closing in fast, but something was wrong. Jasper and Horace seemed to be *sinking*! The rotted stairs were giving way under the carpet runner. And the rug was pulling a cabinet toward the edge of the landing.

Suddenly the carpet slipped from beneath the cabinet. With a dusty *fwoomp* Horace and Jasper dropped through the staircase. A second later Wizzer heard a crashing noise of wood breaking and what sounded like dishes shattering.

As Wizzer watched, the cabinet doors opened, and a hundred heavy glass paperweights fell out. Like colorful bowling balls they thundered down the steps, then fell through the hole. Wizzer hoped every one of them hit Horace and Jasper on the head.

Then he noticed that the cabinet was still teetering on the landing edge. Kipper was barking for the puppies to run down the upstairs hall, but Wizzer couldn't resist. Trotting over to the cabinet, he gave it a little nudge with his nose.

Take that, you mousetrap puppy teaser, he thought. The cabinet rocked for a moment, then crashed down the stairs and landed across the hole. The muffled sound of silverware falling floated up to Wizzer. Laughing to himself, he ran up the stairs.

31

Kipper led the puppies down the hallway. Toward the end of the hall there was a big hole in the floor. The puppies walked carefully around it and into what had once been the laundry room. One of its windows had fallen away, leaving a large opening to the outside. Snow was blowing in, and the room was freezing cold. A water pipe had burst, creating a frozen lake over the floor.

Across the room another door stood open, showing the attic stairs. The line of puppies slid and slipped across the icy floor. They moved through the doorway and up the steps. In the attic, they followed Kipper's footprints in the dust.

In one wall of the attic, a small door led to the roof. Kipper nudged it open. Outside it was cold, dark, and windy. Snow swirled around the roof peaks and chimneys. Kipper leaned over the roof edge and barked.

Wizzer heard an answering bark. It was another member of the rescue team!

6

The Escape

Quickly Kipper explained the plan. The puppies would slide down the roof into a gutter. The gutter's drainpipe would drop them safely to the ground below, where Kipper's friend Fogey was waiting to help them.

As the first puppies began sliding toward the gutter, Wizzer wondered where Horace and Jasper were. He'd better go check around downstairs.

Wizzer trotted past the line of puppies in the attic and down the attic stairs. He slid across the laundry room and shivered—the ice felt awful beneath his paws. At the top of the stairs, he heard the bad men again.

"It's your great bulk that caused the last mess," Jasper was saying.

Wizzer turned and ran back down the hall, stepping around the hole in the floor.

"I ain't taking any more lip from you," Horace replied.

"Quit your whining," Jasper snapped. "We have ninety-nine stinking dogs to catch."

The sound of their voices followed Wizzer down the hall. On the other side of the hole in the floor, he turned to face his attackers. He had to buy Kipper and the others more time.

Jasper spotted him from the other end of

the hallway. Grinning evilly, he lunged toward Wizzer. Wizzer held his ground.

"Come here, you speckled lap rat," Jasper sang, charging down the hall. Too late, he spotted the huge hole. His arms turning like windmills, he skidded toward the hole and dropped through. Wizzer crept closer and peeked over the edge. *Crash!*

Just then one of the hallway doors flung open, and Horace rushed out. He shone his flashlight up and down the hallway.

Wizzer turned and raced for the laundry room. With Horace pounding behind him, Wizzer hit the icy floor and skidded across the room. It was too late to make it to the attic stairs! Wizzer hunched down and closed his eyes, waiting for Horace's blow.

When Horace reached the room, he

shone his flashlight over the floor. "Where've you gone to, you rotten . . . ?"

Wizzer held his breath. A faint bark coming from upstairs made him open one eye. Kipper?

Horace turned away from the laundry room. He hadn't spotted Wizzer! Wizzer got to his feet and crept over to the broken wall. He looked out, wondering if he could jump from the second story to the ground. It looked like a very long way.

Kipper's growl made Wizzer turn. Kipper was in the attic doorway. He'd come back for him! The older dog ordered Wizzer up the attic stairs right away.

Wizzer followed Kipper to the attic door. Kipper bounded up the steps. Right as Wizzer reached the stairs, he turned and gave his angriest yip!

He heard Horace run back to the laundry room. When Horace sounded pretty close, Wizzer wagged his tail at him. *Nyeah, nyeah, nyeah,* he thought.

Kipper's barking sounded from upstairs.

When Horace raced into the laundry room, his feet hit the ice. He fell onto his back with a thud and skidded across the ice like a hockey puck. With a cry of fear he sailed out the broken window, down, down to the frozen pond below.

"Yip! Yip!" Wizzer barked happily. At last he turned and climbed the attic stairs.

Out on the roof, Wizzer scrambled over to Kipper.

"Ruff! Ruff!" Kipper told Wizzer to go down the drainpipe. There was one puppy missing, and he was going back to look for her.

With a final good-bye to Kipper, Wizzer slid down the roof and into the drainpipe. Would he ever see Kipper again?

7

A Cross-country Journey

Wizzer tumbled down the cold metal drainpipe and landed in a soft pile of snow. All of the puppies, including his brothers and sisters, were waiting at the bottom with Fogey, an old English sheepdog who was a friend of Kipper's.

Wizzer explained where Kipper was, and Fogey decided they just couldn't wait for him. Already they could hear a powerful car's engine roaring up the long drive. More trouble! A horn blared as Fogey led the puppies across the wide driveway to a field on the other side. Sweeping headlights, like evil eyes, shone over the snow.

A rotted wooden fence, dripping with icicles, edged the driveway. Fogey helped the puppies through, and they ran across the field. A low stone fence bordered the field, and the puppies jumped over it in a black-and-white spotted stream. Beyond the fence were a flock of thick-wooled white sheep.

A sports car had pulled up in the mansion driveway. From where he hid beneath the toasty-warm fleece of a nice sheep, Wizzer peeked out. Even from across the field, he could see a thin woman sitting inside the car. She had hair that was white on one side of her head and black on the other. This was . . . he knew this human. She was . . . Cruella! Cruella De Vil! She must be the one behind this whole puppy-napping plan.

Wizzer shivered, and not from the cold.

Fogey stood casually by the sheep. After all, he was a sheepdog. Cruella stared at him. Finally she rolled up her car window, backed

down the driveway, and drove off.

Slowly the sheep moved aside, and Wizzer and all the other puppies came out from beneath their warm wool.

With a sharp bark, Fogey ordered the puppies onward, across the snow, and through the dark, cold night.

It felt as if they ran for hours. The cold seeped through Wizzer's short, soft fur. His

paws felt like numb cubes of ice. Wind whistled in his ears and he squeezed his eyes shut. Jewel ran beside him, crying softly. Wizzer tried to keep an eye on his brothers and sisters, making sure no one was lost in the snow and wind.

Just when Wizzer's legs felt as if they would give way beneath him, Fogey barked that they had reached their first stop. Ahead of them was a low, dark building. It was a barn where some friends of his lived. The puppies could rest there for a while.

Inside, Fogey asked some of his friends, who were cows, to provide a snack for the puppies. The puppies had to take turns, and it was very hard for Wizzer to wait. Finally he could share in some of the warm milk, and he drank and drank as much as he could. It felt like years since he had eaten one of Nanny's dinners, though it was only yesterday.

Wizzer was still drinking greedily when he heard a dog barking loudly.

It was Mom! Mom and Dad had found them somehow. He knew they would come! Wizzer pulled away from the cow, burped, then raced with his brothers and sisters to their mother and father.

The other puppies peeped out of the

barn stalls, looking at Pongo and Perdy. Wizzer's parents were amazed. Wizzer quickly explained how they found all the other puppies at the mansion.

Pongo and Perdy called them over. Dozens of Dalmatians spilled out of every corner of the barn and rushed over to Wizzer's parents. Wizzer felt so proud.

Several hours later, after all the puppies had eaten and rested, Fogey jumped to his feet. He barked an alarm, and Pongo and Perdy scrambled out of the stalls where they had been getting filled in on the puppies' adventures.

After a quick look outside, Pongo and Perdy began to herd the puppies through the barn. Cruella De Vil was coming. It was time for another escape.

8

Safe at Last

The puppies squeezed through a hole in the barn wall. Although they were still tired, resting had helped a lot. Wizzer ran proudly next to his dad, toward the back of the group. Perdy was in the lead, and all of the other puppies were in between.

Behind them, Fogey and his friends, the other barn animals, were dealing with Cruella

De Vil. Once Wizzer glanced back just in time to see Cruella crash through a high window and sail into the pigsty. He growled to himself. She deserved everything she got.

Pongo and Perdy led the puppies along the main road, toward town. Wizzer still worried about Horace and Jasper showing up, but Pongo told him that they had been taken care of. Wizzer wished he had seen it.

It wasn't far to town. Wizzer's legs were just starting to get tired when he came to the top of a hill and saw the village lights below.

He asked his father what all the flashing lights were. Pongo told him they were police cars. He figured Roger and Anita had called in the police to help find them. Wait till they saw the puppies—all of them!

Wizzer liked police cars, he decided. They had bright flashing lights and radios. There was plenty of lights and noise and action. What an adventure! Best of all, he was back with his mom and dad.

One of the policemen walked over. "I come up with ninety-eight pups. The two adults make it one hundred even."

Another officer nodded, then clicked his

radio on. "We've got one hundred here, sir."

One hundred Dalmatians, Wizzer thought proudly. Roger and Anita would be so pleased.

Perdy stood up and looked down the road. She barked once. Wizzer ran over to her and followed her gaze. It was Kipper! Kipper had made it! And he was carrying the missing puppy by the scruff of her neck!

"Make that one hundred and one Dalmatians, sir!" the officer said into the radio.

The only times Wizzer had ridden in a car was when the humans had taken the puppies to the vet for their shots. He decided he liked riding in a police car much better. Pongo, Perdy, and Wizzer and his fourteen brothers and sisters all headed back to London together. The remaining puppies filled six other cars. They made a grand parade.

Pongo rolled down his window and barked, sending a message to everyone who had helped him rescue the puppies. He thanked them for their bravery. Wizzer hoped Fogey and the cows and everyone else heard his dad. Wizzer would miss all his new friends.

Back in London, the police took them straight to Roger and Anita's house. The car door opened, and Pongo hopped out, followed by the puppies and Perdy. Roger and Anita hurried out of the house, with Nanny right behind them. Wizzer was so happy to see them! It was great to be home.

"Pongo, old boy! Perdy!" said Roger happily.

"The puppies!" Anita cried.

"The puppies, indeed," said Nanny.

Roger turned to the policemen. "Thank you, gentlemen. We'll be forever grateful."

The police tipped their hats, got into their car, and pulled away. Wizzer scrambled up the steps with his family, hurrying to see what kind of snack Nanny had prepared for them. He heard another car pulling up. Must be the rest of the puppies, he thought.

Wizzer looked out. Sure enough, the other police cars were lined up, and all the puppies were jumping out.

"We can't," Anita said. "We don't have room. Roger, please."

"We'll work something out," Roger said. "We'll get a bigger place."

More and more puppies jumped out of

the cars and swarmed up the steps. Nanny started hugging and kissing them.

"We have seventeen as it is," said Nanny. "What's a few more?"

Anita looked down at Perdy. "You'll have dozens of children, you know."

Perdy nodded yes.

"I won't have them chewing up the carpets and barking at all hours of the night."

Perdy shook her head no.

Finally Anita said, "Everybody inside. Breakfast is getting cold."

Wizzer jumped up and down happily. All of his new brothers and sisters were staying!

9

A Year Later

The scent of blooming flowers tickled Wizzer's nose. He was a young dog now, a year and a half old. The humans—Roger, Anita, their baby, and Nanny—were relaxing on the lawn of their huge new country home. Pongo and Perdy were sleeping in the grass nearby. Wizzer liked the country better than London. There was plenty of room for everybody—space to run around, rabbits to chase, butterflies to jump after . . . And now that Roger and Anita had fixed up the old De Vil mansion, it was a nice place to live.

"I can barely believe it," Roger said dreamily from his chair. "The baby's a year old. We have a new house. A new life."

"We have each other," Anita said.

Wizzer yawned and rolled over.

"We have Nanny," Roger said.

"And I have the two of you," Nanny added fondly.

"We have two wonderful dogs," Roger went on.

Wizzer looked up lazily and saw the rest of his family bounding toward them.

"And they have their children." Anita smiled.

"And their stepchildren," Nanny said.

"And their children have children," Anita said.

"And their stepchildren have children," Roger pointed out.

Opening one eye, Wizzer saw thousands of spotted Dalmatians playing on the grass and in the garden.

"And that reminds me," said Nanny, looking at Anita.

"Roger, darling," Anita said with a smile. "I have wonderful news . . ."

Wizzer rolled over again. He liked the country.